MARY PARKS
PRIVATE INVESTIGATOR

The Lettuce Caper! Live to Die!

All inquiries should be addressed to:

Book Domain LLC.
543 E Louise Dr Phoenix, Az 85050

Ordering Information:
Amount Deals. Special rebates are accessible on the amount bought by corporations, associations, and others. For points of interest, contact the distributor at the address above.

Printed in the United States of America.

ISBN-13   Paperback   978-1-964100-73-9
             eBook   978-1-964100-72-2

Library of Congress Control Number: 2025905787

MARY PARKS
PRIVATE INVESTIGATOR

The Lettuce Caper! Live to Die!

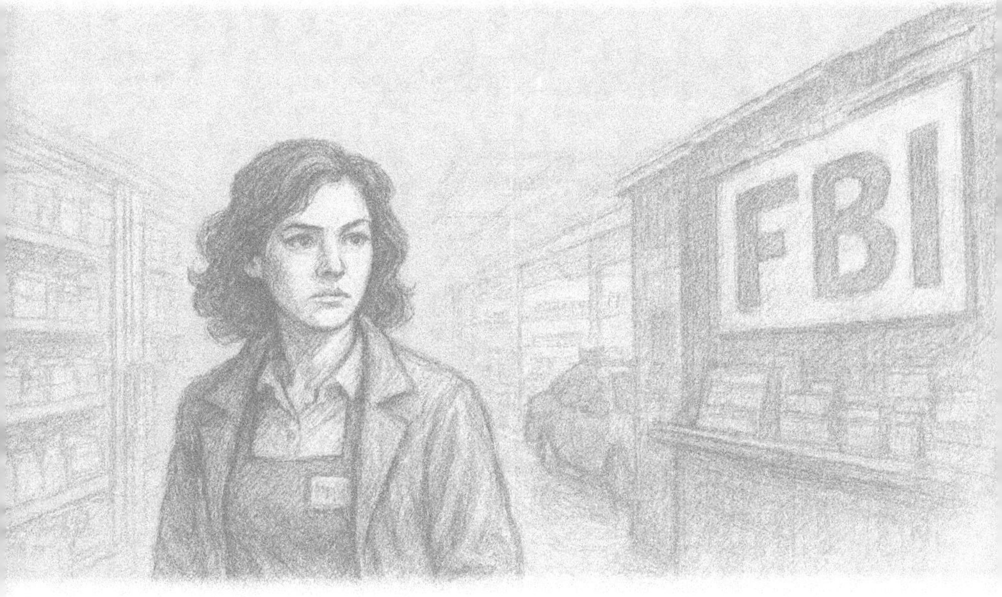

SAM J. CUTRUFELLI

Book 1

Caper 1 The Lettuce Caper

Live to Die

Book 2

Caper 2 The Diamond Caper

Watch for more Mary Park's

Caper Adventures!

CAPER 1

LETTUCE CAPER

My name is Mary Parks, and I am a private investigator or P.I. How that came about is almost uncompromisable. Let me explain. When I finished my high school education, I wanted to sign up as a WAC (Women's Army Corps). I contacted the Army recruiter and set up an appointment. It did not last long though. Within one hour I was told that I had a heart murmur and that was enough to disqualify me or more bluntly put that I had been rejected. I was informed that I could try again in six months and have a doctor monitor my progress. I was given my results and for the doctor a guide as to where I had to be. It was a shattering blow. So back to the drawing board. I had a steady job as a grocery clerk and had been working for the same grocery chain since I was fifteen years old part time about four hours a day while going to school. I am now approaching nineteen years old.

Police work was considered but at this time they were not hiring. The police recruiting officer was a woman and she suggested to me to try Private investigating. She stated that many police officers elected to leave the force and become P.I.'s as they liked the idea of being their own boss and being in business for themselves. It sounded reasonable so I had nothing to lose. Less than forty- eight hours later I was a paid-up rookie P.I. with a diploma and all.

My father and mother did not like the P.I. idea but I convinced them that I would keep working as a grocery clerk and see where the P.I. thing worked out. I put an ad in the local newspaper and to my dismay I got my first job. It was for a one-week assignment. I was hired by an attorney that was representing a woman that suspected that her husband was having an affair. The attorney gave me a zoom camera and told me to snap pictures of anyone going in and out of the woman's residence between the hours of twelve noon to one p.m. This assignment fit in with my regular job schedule. The holidays were coming up, so I had to shelf the P.I. work as the grocery work got to be abnormally busy and we had to work overtime to keep up. Across from the grocery store was a Mom-and-Pop restaurant that was popular with the local businesspeople and I usually went there for lunch. They had a counter with about ten seats plus some tables. I usually sat at the counter to get faster service. One day there was a vacant stool next to mine which was being set-up for a young man. He acknowledged me then asked me "What was good to eat here"? I told him I was having a bacon, lettuce, and tomato (B.L.T.) sandwich. So, he said, "sounds good to me" and then he said his name was Joel and that he was a free-lance reporter. Joel looked incredibly young, so he asked me my name and I said "Marilyn Monroe" and giggled. It did not bother Joel one bit and he said I like a woman that has a sense of humor. So, he started eating his B.L.T. when he yelped out "dam I bit my tongue", Marilyn can you hand me a napkin. So, I guess he probably won that round and to make sure he said, "I'll see you at your station later Mary." He pointed to my name tag on my shirt that said very clearly MARY. I liked him. Joel was as he said a free-lance reporter, but he was also an undercover F.B.I. agent. Very few people knew this as with other undercover agents their life depended upon their amenity. He was here because the F.B.I. got a sniff of something irregular happening and it was the way they operated, put together little bits and pieces and sometimes they develop into something more. What happened took place about two a.m. yesterday morning. A lone person was trying to break and enter the grocery store that Mary Parks worked at. He had a Jimmie bar that he was using to try to pry the door open. Suddenly he knew the gig was up as he heard a car come screeching into the parking lot with no lights on. It must be a silent alarm that went off and they were investigating it. The only thing he could do was to get rid of his Jimmie bar, so he threw it behind a nearby bush, he also had a small duffel bag with assorted tools which he managed to throw behind the same bush. There were three men that got out of the car they had guns and very powerful flashlights. They grabbed the would-be burglar and asked what he was up to, the man was a quick thinker and he said he had to urinate when he went to do his business, he frightened some guy probably a homeless, that ran off than you came. So, they searched him and found a wallet plus a small gun. They removed all his possessions, watch, ring and then shot him with a silencer and took off. When the authorized alarm people arrived, they found him dead. Around the corner they also found the night watchman that was also shot by another group in another car, but he was not dead yet but was losing the battle. The local police arrived, and the ambulance also arrived. It was bedlam with all the activity going on. The F.B.I. usually does not get involved but there was another incident that coincided at about the same time and the two incidents might be tied together. So, the first incident was the break in, where they recovered a sheet of paper in a duffel bag that said "let" just one word, so the F.B.I. ran the word through their vast system and it kept coming up with the word "lettuce". The second incident was off the coast of Santa Cruz, California, and it was huge. It involved a collision of a large merchant vessel and a passenger fishing boat plus the murder of at least eight to ten people. Three armed men boarded the fishing boat and rounded up the crew of six, five men and one woman. The six were handcuffed and their legs were shackled together than they put tape across their mouths. They were put in the boats fishing net and the one apparently the head man started the heavy winch that had a long boom attached. The net loaded with live people was extended over the ocean.

The winch malfunctioned and the human cargo was stuck about twenty feet up in the air. The plan was to drop the net into the water. The second man was an explosive expert and he placed four timer activated explosive bags strategically located. When he came back on deck he nonchalantly shot and killed the winch operator. When he faced to kill the third man who figured that is when the winch operator was killed, he would be next, so he was prepared. Apparently, they wanted no witnesses because dead men do not talk. The fishing boats radar picked up a huge entity on their screen. It was determined to be a large boat. A collision was imminent and unavoidable. The captain of the merchant ship ordered maneuvers, but it was too late the momentum would keep them moving forward. The captain ordered all lifeboats to be lowered for life saving operations, but the two vessels collided with a thunderous blast scattering the lighter fishing boat in half. Then there was the deafening blast as the explosives set off. The merchant vessel had a gaping hole on the side and the captain ordered SOS radioed out but for the time being he did not order an evacuation. The collision of the merchant vessel and the fishing boat was not accidental but a planned collision. The incident is still an ongoing FBI case so if the facts are not available what will we know. The merchant vessel and the fishing boat were both part of the cocaine group. The cocaine organization was exceptionally large and well organized, and they discovered that the crew of the fishing boat was pilfering their profits, so they had to be eliminated. Hence the phony collision, but things went wrong, and they handcuffed and shackled the crew so if they were found secured as they were it would suggest murder and further not an accident. In the real-world things happen.

The third man then abandoned the fishing boat that was headed towards the mother boat and anchored about two miles away. When he got near the mother boat two men with high powered rifles started shooting at him, so he dove into the water. He had two tanks strapped to his back plus a scuba mask. An observant crew member told the captain of the mother boat and about the tanks so they figured out how far he could get with his supply. So, he ordered for the ground people to patrol and intercept him and kill him on sight. They did intercept him, and they did start shooting at him. He got shot but could maneuver so he evaded capture for the moment. He had a safe house nearby it was a small cottage on the beach, so he headed to it. He was an undercover agent for one of the other world crime organizations. He managed to get the radio going and was able to send out one word "lettuce" before he was killed. So, the word "lettuce" was once again on all the air waves but what did it mean? Amid all the tragedy Joel and Mary got to know each other well. They were not exactly a twosome from it all but they enjoyed their friendship. Joel suggested to his controller that they should hire Mary as she was already inside, and they suspected the store was one of the keys to the lettuce caper. So, the FBI thought it was a good idea and Mary was told how they wanted her to act plus there was a wage aspect of the job. The FBI was very free with their money. The money was not the object when you are dealing with hundreds of millions of dollars, plus how many addictions although at the time they had no proof that narcotics were really involved.

Thinking back, Joel thought it was odd that a private group was set up to tap into the grocery alarm system as they were able to arrive at the break in of the grocery store before the personnel from the alarm company. The grocery chain Mary worked for had four stores, three besides where Mary worked. Joel figured that maybe this whole mess was bigger than they first anticipated. So again, Joel related all his thoughts to his controller adding, I think we should stake a mock break in and see if the private alarm people were monitoring the other three stores but to avoid suspicion, they could only do this at one of the other three, the question was which one? The FBI decided to go with the chains newest and biggest store. The alarm people the legitimate company managed to adjust the alarm to be very sensitive so that the FBI guy could set it off before the alarm people came was the plan. The idea worked beautifully so when the bogus cars came screeching into the parking lot it was empty, so they figured it was a false alarm and left. So as Joel thought, this was a very big and well-organized operation. What they were doing was still conjecture but probably narcotics was involved, but why the grocery store angle? And are all four stores involved? So, the FBI checked each and every person in the store's employment including the store's owners. So now they had a fairly good lead. A few more breaks were needed before they had a definite path that break would come next week. Charles Regold was Mary's supervisor at the grocery store. He was going on a short skiing trip with his girlfriend who was half his age. Charles was a married man with two children but love or lust or both led Charles into a seemingly familiar pattern some call it the middle age syndrome, regardless of the why and wherefore this path usually leads into some wanted and unwanted paths. Charles's assistant manager was young, able and he would be acting manager while Charles was vacationing, but things change. He was an avid hiker and somehow an insect got into his boot and he is now in the hospital fighting the possible loss of his leg from the poisonous insect bite. So, Mary was the next in line. Normally in an emergency the skiing trip would have been cancelled, but the allure of what was before him was beyond common sense as he said to his superiors that Mary was fully capable to fill in also, he would be checking in with her every two or three times a day. So, late Saturday Charles drove off with his mistress in tow. Mary was to be the manager for one week. Mary was told by Charles to do the preparatory work for the new construction that was to be a big improvement to the overall store's growth. So, Mary called the contractor and told them that Charles was on a week vacation and that he would like some preliminary work done and when he returned, they would go forward until completed. The contractor said he would send two men immediately. That was done the next order of importance was to contact her controller at the FBI and advise them to start work on the six security cameras that were to be installed in the office that Charles used when working on matters concerning ordering supplies. The plan was to have four or five professional electronics experts install small cameras to monitor Charles. It was to be done very professionally as Charles was very aware of the slightest of change. So, shortly after that the electronics men arrived. Estimated time would be two days if there were no hang-ups. Then as soon as you think everything is falling in place disaster looms. Murphy's law was in place. When you least expect disaster expect it. It will be there. The owners of the store were notified that Charles had a skiing accident. The police report said he was intoxicated and skiing under abnormal weather conditions, skiing downhill and he hit a tree. He did not hit his head luckily, but his body hit the side of the tree. He was taken to the hospital. He had a broken right arm, badly dangled but not broken and a left-hand wrist injury. Shoulder and hip bruises with possible implications. Charles would be hospitalized two days and he should be back by Wednesday. The police and hospital staff said he had a money belt in place with over twenty-five thousand dollars. So now the construction people where really being pushed, another man helped but the area was small and all five could not work at one time they also would work twenty-four hours straight if they were getting behind. Mary finally got a break they were keeping Charles for one more day for further x-rays and observations. Whew! They lucked out but the operation lettuce is still going nowhere fast or slow. Until they get a break. It is a stale mate. Joel had some observations and a plan that he presented to this controller. First there was no way the FBI could inspect the hundreds of cases of lettuce without giving up their plan.

Secondly, he thought that the operation was relatively small so he figured the transporters would be small to suit. It was inconceivable that a small ship would use the mammoth facilities at the San Francisco main dock but would seek to use one of the smaller docks. Question was which one? Although the smaller ship could use these docks, they could not bring in enough goods per trip to handle a large part of the coast so Joel figured they had to have a way of marking the cases so that they could be segregated from the rest of the shipment. That is if they were smuggling the narcotics via the lettuce crate theory. Joel's plan was to stage a mock escape of two or three criminals and use that as an excuse to seal off the incoming ships by buoys and just have one entry and one exit. It would be a slow process, but it was better than doing nothing but watch grass grow. Charles was back to work he was measurable, but his arm was in a cast, he could move his fingers. On the other side his wrist was just sprained so it was not in a cast and his hand was sprained but he could maneuver it. So, goes for Charles, His girlfriend signed for his clothes and belonging at the hospital but since then she has disappeared along with his money belt of twenty-five thousand dollars and his wallet that had five thousand dollars in it. She drove his car to Reno and abandoned it. The assistant manager died from his insect bite. He left a wife and one child. The cameras in Charles second office were working fine but no significant happenings so far. Charles called the dock superintendent and proposed that he talk to the head of the FBI man monitoring the cordoned off area. He told him he needed fifteen cases of lettuce and some other vegetables for the hospital in the area. The captain agreed and notified Joel's controller. This was a step forward, now if ever they would have a better chance of inspecting fifteen cases of lettuce versus hundreds of cases. Charles could not drive in the condition, so he asked Mary to get the stores long bed pickup and drive him to the dock to get the crates of lettuce. When they arrived at the dock, three cases of lettuce were stacked apart from the other twelve. While Charles was conversing with the dock supervisor, Mary took pictures of the crates especially the separated three. The dock superintendent came with one longshore man and they loaded Mary's truck and he and Charles instructed an employee to bring the three cases to his office and put the others in the cooler room. An expert computer man was sent to transfer the photos from her cellphone to his computer. His van was a complete computer workshop. They did this while Charles went to his second office. The computer man told Mary she did fine as the photos were noticeably clear and readable. Charles finally came to Mary and asked her to drive him to the other two stores as he wanted to talk with the managers about how business was and if they needed any improvements. This time Mary took the managers private car. Each time they reached a store the Manager and Charles would tell Mary to sit and wait that he would not be long. Each time he took his small satchel with him. When Mary got a chance, she called her controller who congratulated her on the fine work that she was doing, but nothing of real use as of yet. Mary interrupted and said the three cases show a dot in the center of the letter "e" in lettuce and the other cases there were no dots on the letters "e." He said Mary, I think you just solved this case! I am looking at the photos now and now I see it. Mary you are a winner and if this solves the case, I am going to reward your purse strings with getting you a bonus! Now it became clear what Charles did in his second office. He opened each case and inside there was ten pouches of what looked like quality cocaine. He carefully opened each bag and removed a teaspoonful which he parceled out into four cellophane bags, one for each store manager and one for the dock supervisor. As smart as Charles thought he was his cocaine organizations people were smarter. When they picked up the three pouches and took them to their headquarters each sack was weighted on precision scales made specifically for the U.S. Postal service. It was evident that each pouch was tampered with and a quantity removed. Later that day they went to Charles's apartment, but he was found dead, he had been strangled to death. We also found that the dock supervisor had been drowned and his body washed ashore, and his hands and feet had been bound together. The one manager had left his store and was never to ever be seen again. Manager two was also found dead in his office as an apparent suicide. As far as the lettuce caper goes, it was done for, but the organization was just too large and was noted to be worldwide. The loss of the lettuce operation would hurt a little but would be restarted with new players. It was business as usual after a slight pause. Joel was given a large bonus and Mary also received a large bonus.

Mary was offered the store manager position, but she declined, but her bosses gave her a substantial reward. Mary and Joel's relationship continued to blossom and maybe bloom into something else.

The end.

LIVE TO DIE CAPER!

$\mathcal{B}$ ucks Road was a two-lane road that started at the head of the town and divided it into two halves, then went on to the next town and did the same. It was no different when it came to the city of Singlebury. That road divided and kept going on and on. By all appearances appear to be a small sleepy city but, it was quite huge. The town itself is small which included a bank, a grocery store and a post office and a single pump gas station, plus some smaller buildings. After you left the town, Singlebury was in his element with large tracts of land and hundreds of acres each covered the landscape. There were huge cattle ranches for most part but occasionally a small parcel that was a vegetable farm or fruit tree farm but mostly they were large cattle ranches.

The Jefferson Ranch was by far the largest. It was started by Israel Jefferson and succeeded by his son Rory who had two sons that succeeded him they were Russell and Jeffrey Jefferson. Russell was now the family rancher as Jeffrey the other son was not interested at all or for that matter in ranching in general. His interest was geology studying the land mostly oil tracks, so he and Russell had a working agreement regarding the ranch and its daily work programs to keep the ranch workable and profitable. So naturally the two brothers went their separate ways. Jeffrey loved the vast potential of Texas so that is where he migrated to. Russell Jefferson stayed on at the ranch. Russell lost his wife early on he never remarried. He was advertising for a husband-and-wife team to oversee the Jefferson family home that was separate from the cattle ranch. It was about fifteen acres fenced off from the ranch with a huge two-story home plus assorted cottages for guests. The main house had a three-bedroom addition attached to the main house but not part of it. It was basically used by the overseer and his family which at this time was Mr. and Mrs. Meeks. Rosenda Meeks and Jaycee Meeks. Rosenda was nineteen years old and of Hawaii in heritage, she was not exceptionally pretty but not ugly by any means.

Mr. Meeks was also Hawaiian and about forty-five years of age and a former Hawaii and Army man. His function in the Army was in the motor pool, servicing the camp vehicles but his many allergies interfered, and he was discharged on a medical discharge and was given a small pension. The Meeks were settled in nicely at the ranch and Rosenda became pregnant and delivered a son and named him Ralph Meeks. Ralph was not an extremely healthy little boy and at the the small age his health became worse meanly due to his asthma attacks but in general the Meeks and the Jefferson's got along very well. When Ralph was four years old, he wanted a pair of boots, so Mrs. Meeks drove into town where two brothers had a shoe business.

The older brother, Mr. Holmes was a hat blocker and cleaner. His business was good because almost every male had a Stetson hat for Sunday to wear to church must be blocked and clean. His brother worked as a bootmaker in Nevada and was incredibly talented, but his big drawback was that he was totally deaf, but he was so good that his employer put up with his deficiencies. His employer died and his wife wanted nothing to do with the shoe business, so she sold the equipment to Jimmy. Jimmy was to move the equipment to a more desirable location but that never matured so it was to be sold in the lock stock and barrel had to be moved. The store next to Mr. Holmes hat shop with vacant so everything was moved to Singlebury, Arizona. The two stores were combined into one with some remodeling. It was a nice set up for Jimmy's hearing. When Mr. Holmes was not too busy, he can help his brother with customers but that was sell them. So, Mrs. Meeks and Ralph went in the home store to buy his boots but there was a customer having trouble communicating to Jimmy what it was he wanted. They were both getting agitated when Mrs. Meeks interrupted and explained with drawings and sign language what the customer wanted. It ended favorably for Jimmy and the customer. So, Mr. Holmes asked Mrs. Meeks if she could devote some time each day to help Jimmy. She was demure and said she would think it over. About three months later she announced that she was pregnant. The ranch was running smoothly. One of the cowboys had a rather severe fall when his horse stumbled so Mr. Jefferson asked him to help Mr. Meeks as he appeared to be faltering. His wife was to help Rosenda Meeks. Two months later Mr. Meeks died.

This change would change the Jefferson Ranch forever. One day, Mr. Jefferson received a phone call from his neighbor saying that the neighbor wanted to sell his ranch and a Mr. Jefferson was interested. An appointment was made. Normally Mr. Jefferson would go to the top of his property along the main road then to his neighbors but this time he decided to go to the center of his ranch, and he can be at a gate in the fence opening on to the neighbors' ranch. Suddenly his horse stopped almost throwing Mr. Jefferson. Mr. Jefferson asked the horse what the matter is and to continue, but the horse would not move. Mr. Jefferson dismounted and saw a dozen pools of what appeared to be muddy water, so he inspected further, and he smelled the water and it smelled oily and felt oily. He had never been around oil in the ground, so he decided to call his brother who was a geologist in Texas and discuss the problem. He then walked his horse from the area and continue to meet with his neighbor. After having pie and coffee they started discussing business. When all is said and done, Mr. Jefferson agreed to the price but told Jim Burns about the ordeal and how his horse was not wanting to proceed further. So, he told Mr. Burns that if he had oil possibly Mr. Burns would likely also have oil. Mr. Jefferson said he was calling his brother tomorrow and he would talk to him further. He thanked Mr. Burns for the pie and coffee and left.

The following day he called Gregory in Texas. Mrs. Jefferson, Gregory's wife answered and after the necessary talk he was told Gregory was in Saudi Arabia. She would call him and ask Gregory to contact his brother. Gregory called him and listened to his brother's experience and he told his brother well it sounds suspicious like an oil pool. I will call my friend who owns an oil refinery close by and have them come and look. I will be back home in about three weeks so hang in there and we will go from there. Josh Price, Gregory's friend, came to look at the area and he said yes, it is oil, how much I do not know until we take some drillings, but I guess it is a bundle. Gregory came over to look and he took some preliminary findings, and he told his brother that he thought he hit a mother lode of oil. We are rich now but if I am right, we are ultra-rich. We will just have to play it along by the way your friend, the neighbor will also share in our wealth. You did right by him big brother. It ended up with Jefferson's Cattle Ranch was now called Jefferson's Cattle Ranch and Oil Field. Five high quality oil producing rigs were in place and Jefferson and just release the remainder of the land on a percentage deal. Ralph was practically grown now he was sixteen years old. Ralph is always kind of sickly where as Wordin with a ball of energy and never sick. Their mother was in Germany, so Wordin occasionally would write to her and he would tell her how Ralph and he missed her and their father. So, then he would ride his beloved three-wheel sidecar motorbike to town where he would send the letter on its way. Wordin liked Mrs. Pearson because she would take the time to talk to the younger customers. She owned the grocery store in town plus there was a corner that was an official post office plus outside she had a single gas pump. The only gas in town. Mrs. Pearson asked Wordin if he could service the truck that had just pulled in. Wordin was only too glad to help. The kid that was the service station attendant moved with his family to California so at the present time there was no gas attendant. Mrs. Pearson was used to the downs of owning a business, but the gas pump is leaving plus the mail carrier also leaving was a little much. So, she asked Wordin if he would like the job. He was pleased as he liked to stretch his capabilities to the limit. So, he would start tomorrow at four a.m. and work the route with the post man until he left. The job was a split shift job. The city mail was delivered in the morning and the rule area was covered in the afternoon. There was a gap between shifts of two and one-half to three hours so he would help by doing the gas pump. Mrs. Pearson was grateful as to give him time to repair flat and sneak in some food. Time flew by as it was three years ago when he became the city and county mail carrier. Each morning he would buy two boxes of suckers plus a box of chocolate covered candy bar. Everyone on his route liked him and he liked his job. Then catastrophe hit, and it hit hard. It was going to be a day that would never be forgotten. It started with a cold cold rain which was not happy but terrifying as most electrical rains were generally large explosions of flashlight that lit up the sky plus loud thunder is shaking thunder. To make it worse the truck to pick up and deliver the mail to the post office somehow delivered the wrong mail to Mrs. Pearson. It would be a three-hour delay for him until they resolve the issue. So, he decided to go home. Driving home he experienced a feeling of finality. Every hair on his body was going but his concentration was to not get sloppy in this control of his bike, so the dreaded experience past. In the meantime, Ralph and Wordin 's wife of a little over one year were having some similar experiences. They were setting up a big surprise for Wordin, but each day well canceled say it just does not feel right. I am not clairvoyant, but everything tells you to stop. Just then they heard Wordin's motorbike pumping up the incline. The horse stall was spooked at every electrical bolt from loud thunder noise, he would kick and hammer his body against the stall door trying to break for freedom. Wordin drove right into his usual parking spot. Ralph was waiting for him with a double edge axe above his head. The horse finally knocked his door open and escaped for freedom through the open door. In doing that he brushed up against Ralph with such force that Ralph was knocked over and it was enough to hamper his swing. The judgment was enough to split Wordin's head wide open at the right temple, so his head was hinged, and the skin was flapping. Wordin was nearly unconscious, but he was strong and when Ralph tried for a second hitting blow Wordin caught the axe handle. Ralph was much weaker than Wordin and he had to let go of the axe but Wordin swung the axe and it hit him under the leg and down Ralph went. Then Wordin with a mighty swing decapitated his brother. In a matter of seconds, the murder was murdered. Born to die! Then he heard Lori whimpering and he said "you too and sit down" blood and gore all over him. "I loved Ralph now I'm a murderer for life and you are an adulterous for life." "Leave now before I kill you." The sheriff will be over and tell him that I left you and you very seldom see Ralph. He then loaded Ralph onto the motorbike driver's seat and buckled him in and drove off. Then he returned and cleaned the axe and put it in the tool barrel. He got a sack of corn and spread it all over the area. He got along side of the bike and drove up the hill. He heard a whimper and would sounded like a meow as he passed a bush, he saw that it was a little totally wet girl and her kitten he stood her up and asked what she was doing in the rain with only her nightgown on? She said she was searching for her little kitten. Wordin reached in his pocket for two suckers, here is one for you and one for your little kitten now you get home, and you get dry clothes on and get warm and get into bed. Wordin then poured gasoline all over Ralph and the motorbike and pushed it to the edge of the road. Rolled up some papers and lit them. He threw the flammable paper on the gas and off it went. A good shove and it went tumbling down the incline. He had another gas can of full of gas that he grabbed and proceeded to follow the animal trail down to the fire. Just to make sure he threw the full can of gas on the fire. He got to the hill towards the road about halfway when he saw a Jeep enter the canyon and stop.

Two men and a dog were approaching them probably the Sherriff or the county police. The dog smelled or heard him, so he started barking and snarling. Wordin stayed motionless but once the dog got his scent he would not stop acting up until he investigated. Presently the Jeep took off with one man and the dog. Worden then started scampering up the slope. He reached the top at about the same time as the Jeep. He then put a revolver in each hand as the dog was released. Worden was extremely calm when the dog got close enough, it shot it three times with his left hand then he shot the driver who was aiming to shoot him with a rifle. Then Wordin took off, he knew every trail in these parts and he headed for a concealed animal trail that the animals used to get to the water in the river below. Jordin ran through the light rain and the darkness; he was able to make his escape. Dogs were useless because the wet covered up his scent. He crossed the river at a low point then headed toward a concealed refuge he used as a kid. Worden knew he had to get out of the area when daylight came because the police would be everywhere just like ants. A helicopter would also be employed, but for now he had to rest. His head felt like he had a ton of bricks on his shoulders. Maybe it is infected? He found his hideout and moved right in. He would be able to see the train when the time came, he would then hop it and be gone. If only his head did not hurt so bad. Finally, he heard the train struggling to get up to the top of the incline and when the train reached the top it started to gain speed, so Wordin grabbed a holding bar and scrambled into an empty box car. The trip would be short as the train stopped for hours to load and unload but at least he would be gone from here. He decided to get as far away from town as they probably would search the train. Enter Mary Parks, she received a call from Mr. Jefferson. Mary said that she was Mary Parks, so Roger Jefferson began speaking. This morning at the hours between three and five a.m. an accident or possible accident occurred when a three wheeled motorcycle sidecar went off the road with a driver in it and it caught on fire. It was an extremely hot fire and the coroner said it would be some time to determine all the facts. I would like to retain you and your associate, Kristi. My reasons are very personal. You will receive a non-refundable check for twenty-five thousand dollars, plus your nonrefundable fee, each employee will receive current wage plus a 10% bonus. Plus, all Parks PI firm's daily operating expenses. For three months or if we have a sooner closure than that will be an extra 10%. If you agree to this, I will hire a jet to pick you up at the airport in California. A chauffeur car would take you to the area within an hour if agreeable. I have a very spacious home you can call yours while employed. I will supply all necessary vehicles and other expenses to bring this tragedy to a closure. Mary Parks agreed and shortly thereafter the chauffeur driven limousine arrived to take them to the airport. The jet landed in a private airstrip near Jefferson's ranch. A chauffeured limo then took them to Roger Jefferson's ranch. They met Mr. Jefferson who was in a wheelchair. It was ten a.m. so Mr. Jefferson said that they should rest and freshen up then they would have lunch and after lunch they would meet in the assembly room and Mr. Jefferson would relay the whole story. They all met at one thirty p.m. in Jefferson's assembly room and office so Mr.

Jefferson began. You can make notes plus a recording, but it is to be used only for reference to what we speak of. When the three months are up all notes and recordings will be turned over to my lawyer. All memo notes and personal accounts of this week will be given to me. You are working for me and not the police or any other organization. Your findings on a need-to-know platform. If all is agreed I will proceed. Mr. and Mrs. Yee were my father's caretakers of the private part of the Jefferson's cattle ranch. Approximately ten acres were fenced off from the ranch. My grandfather did this so he and his family would have privacy from the ranch. They lived in the three-bedroom apartment attached to the family home. Mr. Yee gave notice to my father that he and his wife were retiring and to search for a husband-and-wife team to take over their job. Before this chance took place, my father passed on, so I was faced with the task of replacing the Yee's. I put an ad in the local rancher's paper advertising for a husband-and-wife team to caretake my property. Surprisingly, we received six responses and after careful consideration I finally chose Mr. and Mrs. Meeks. They both were of Hawaiian descent and Mr. Meeks was a soldier in the army but due to certain allergies, he was being discharged. They needed a month before they could start their new job because of his termination from the Army would take two weeks from the day that we spoke. Mr. and Mrs. Yee had already left but some of the cowboys helped. Things got back to normal. The Meeks were particularly good at their job and we were lucky to have them. Each week on Friday, Mr. Meeks and I met in my office and Mr.

Meeks gave me a written report as to any problems, plus a list of necessary purchases. Before each meeting they had a snack and a brief impersonal chat. This procedure was now about one year old. During our informal talks I told Mr. Meeks about never marrying after my wife and our expected child died. Mr. Meeks confided that he was sterile because of allergies but his wife really wanted children and she was unaware of his impotency. We talked, Mr. and Mrs. Meeks about adoption and other options but nothing transpired. One day Mr. Meeks said he had a business deal to discuss with me, but it could wait until Friday when he gave his progress report. This Friday I had a previous appointment, so I called Mr. Meeks and told him to leave the written report on my desk. His initial request was so brief that I completely forgot about it. We finally met and Mr. Meeks was nervous and kind of embarrassed and he asked if I remembered about discussing a proposal deal. Mr. Meeks continued and stated look I am not getting any younger and my impotency is starting to mess with my marriage. I do not know how to put this, but I wondered if maybe you and her my wife could get together and have a child, a boy child that would be heir for you and as a son for us. No one needs to know it is your child only us three would know of Jaycee's problem. If you think my wife and I are too brash, and you would want to terminate our stay I would not take it personally as I am trying to save my marriage and possibly give you something in return. Please give it some thought. This came out of the blue but maybe it could be worked out. Mr. Meeks and I talked further than Mrs. Meeks said she was too embarrassed and that she did get a little under my skin when she said I want something, and you want something. I do not love you and you do not love me, so it is a boy meets girl; girl had a child it happens every day. At the time I was told that I was living in the past and things have changed but I had not. So, more time passed went fine one day I called Mr. Meeks and said okay let us talk. I owned a small parcel bordering the Jefferson ranch, so the proposal was for Mr. and Mrs. Meeks to move out of the apartment and live on the adjoining property. There was a nice ranch home plus a two-star staple and a three-car carport plus a 1935 Ford sedan and a 1935 Ford coupe and a three-wheel motorcycle with a sidecar. So, there were more personal talks and Rosenda dated she felt she was being shanghaied. Which made Mr. Meeks get very belligerent? As he said to his wife do not act so prissy like before I met you have two miscarriages with two different men so do not act like your virginity is being taken from you and furthermore you suggested this whole shenanigan so if you want out say so and I will apologize to Mr. Jefferson and get on with our life. There was never any talk of money, but I gave Mr. Meeks a check for ten thousand dollars which I am sure they would appreciate. Rosenda had a baby boy name Ralph and Mr. Meeks was the proud father of Ralph Meeks. So, Mary Parks and Christie now let us go further. There was a body in that cycle, and it could be Ralph. You and Christie are the only ones that now know about Ralph and it had to remain so. Ralph and Wordin have both disappeared. The coroner said the fire was so intense that it might be weeks or months before a positive identification could be made. I would like to know sooner than that. I have arranged for you to have any information you might need from the sheriff. A new black SUV will be here within the0 hour for you and Christie to get around in, good luck. Christie was driving and they both agreed to talk to the sheriff and hope some news had come in. The weather was still bad but not stormy it was just cold and drizzling but if you were out in the open you would get wet very quickly. The sheriff was cordial but seemed a little bit miffed that Jefferson suggested he help these two girls, but Jefferson was part of everyone in town so when Jefferson said or suggested something it was like just do it. I had told Mary Parks that there was no further news, and it was only a few hours old that is the case on hand.

He the sheriff told Mary he had a deputy searching the hills with night glasses, but it was too wet and not much help because the night goggles would become useless when wet. He said he saw something like a spark when the lightning hit, he told Mary that he saw something but dismissed it. Mary was not convinced that anything regardless how small should be dismissed. Mary asked the sheriff if the deputy could drive her to the approximate location. Again, the sheriff was miffed but anything to get them off his back. Percy the deputy had a four-wheel covered Jeep, his pride and he held the door open for Mary. He was so very gallant. Mary asked Christie to drive to the grocery, post office and talk to Wordin's employer just to cover all the bases. Percy and Mary had to drive a considerable distance before they could cross the river as it rained hard at times driving at night. In fact, Percy wondered how the fire was so hot and did not extinguish itself. Then he laughed and said that is why I am just a lowly deputy. They passed a small trailer house that Percy said belonged to an old man and woman there patrolling the road checked for damages plus there were three or four railyard sheds that had tools in them my picks and shovels, etc. They seem to always be broken into. They stopped and they got out of the Jeep and they both had raingear on, so they were not going to get wet as it was only just a heavy mist. Percy stopped and picked up a wet aluminum covered candy wrapper. It said Johnson's chocolate bar. Percy said yup Worden was here. Worden loved his candy and lived on it. Soon they found some more wrappers. Mary put on gloves and put the wrappers in a plastic bag. Percy came upon a clump of bushes that were very dense but there was a spot at the base look to be like entrance to the interior of the bush. Percy got on his belly and jiggled his way inside. Mary said holy cow Worden was here there's candy wrappers and bloodshed grain sacks. So, she took out her camera and snapped ten or twelve shots and she told Percy not to touch or move anything. This was a significant finding. It did not prove anything, but it implied a lot. Percy had a radio in his Jeep, and he called the sheriff. The sheriff was excited, and he said good work Percy I will see you get a raise. Percy came back to Mary. Mary wrote out a report from Mr. Jefferson. In one hour, the area was swamped with cops, reporters, and city officials. They all figured that Worden was the prime suspect, but Mary has some questions to ponder on. Worden apparently was injured. Assumption was that Worden held up waiting for the train so he could hop a ride into town, so the sheriff had a APB put out for Worden's arrest that was sent to every law enforcement office in the area.

Jefferson was incredibly pleased with the progress and he told Mary you only get what you pay for, but he was not happy with what the report implied. If Worden is alive where is Ralph, could Ralph be the burn body. Christie congratulated Mary and gave her report what was told to her that Worden was the best postman that ever delivered in the city and County of Singlebury. Worden has started working as a postman at the age of fifteen to sixteen years old and everyone liked him, he gave out candy, suckers to all the children on his route. Many of the post's customers baked cookies and cakes for him. He worked a split shift delivering the city's post first then in the afternoon the county. There was not much more to tell. He was never late only diligent so what more could be said. The little girl that was looking for her kitten told her mother what happened, so the mother called the sheriff. There was so much excitement over Percy and Mary's discovery that the sheriff did not have a person to see Mrs. Yardoff. So, he asked Christie to go see her. This is her story her little girl's name was Camille Yardoff. Camille had told her mother that her little kitten had wandered off and she went to find the kitten outside and she heard a motorcycle climbing their slope from the Meeks house, so she hid among some bushes by the side of the road. The bike stopped when he reached the top. Just then her kitten meowed, and she was probably cold from being wet. The man had found me and the kitten. He asked her her name but that she could barely talk because she was shivering so bad. He asked her where she lived, and she told him she was lost. He gave me two candy suckers one for me and one for my kitten and told me to hurry home as my mother was probably worried sick about me. It was too dark, so I never saw his face, that is all. He was genuinely nice. So, Christie called Lori Meeks, Worden's wife and asked if she could talk to her for a few minutes. Lori said sure, come right over. Christie knocked on the door and was led in by an extremely attractive girl. She was dressed as if she was going to church in all white and not one hair was misplaced. So, they shook hands and Lori guided Christie into the parlor when she Lori had set up two coffee cups and a carafe of coffee. They sipped coffee and had cookies and talked about nothing. I asked Laurie to just relax and tell me what she wanted to say.

Lori said it was genuinely nice for her to let her talk or talk about her story. So, Christie said Lori you are not a suspect we just feel that you are being so close to the incident that you might be helpful to us. Lori said she lived here all her life she was twenty-one years old now. I worked for Mr. Jefferson off and on since I was about twelve years old. I helped in the house, working with Mrs. Yee. My sister is two years older, and she owned a bar restaurant next to the post office. Also, there are six or eight permanent borders so Cheryl, Lori's sister needed some help and so I told Mr. Jefferson it was all good and he told me to go and help Cheryl. We used to live across the Meeks property when I worked there but when Mrs. Meek is coming to live here, she asked me not to cross through her yard. Mr. Meeks was a Jefferson's property caretaker. Meeks worked in the bakehouse and Mr. Jefferson had his cowboy's wife to help Mrs. Meeks. Mr. Jefferson was always thoughtful of his keep. He seemed to be able to handle the need of the big house and Mr. Meeks seemed to handle all the outside part. It made no difference to Mr. Jefferson that now it took two more helpers to do the same job. Mr. Jefferson was a good man. Christie told Mary that Lori is ready to gush out the recent events, but she needed time. Mary asked Christie to arrange a time for the three of them to meet as Mary wanted to meet Lori. Well, that was being all set up Worden was on the train that he had hopped. He was anxious to get far away so he could care for himself as he was an awfully sick man. The hurt was unbelievable. The train slowly past the old Indian squaw's place and Worden remembered that she had showed him how to make a poncho out of a ten-cent piece of plastic.

It was raining hard again so he made his poncho out of the plastic he had in his backpack. He thanked the old Indian squaw to himself. As for a ten-cent idea he would be dry. His plan was to jump off the train a few miles from town as they were probably assuming, he was on the train. Instead of going towards down the backtrack towards the old Indian squaw's place he stayed off the road to follow the animal trails. He was getting close to a trailer when he heard the loud sound of a powerful engine, so Worden crouched down low and waited. It was an ambulance and a pickup heading for the trailer. The two vehicles stopped, and the sheriff appeared at the trailer. Worden was close enough to hear them talk. The sheriff said I did not think it was Meek's boy as he always got along with the Indian. So glad we got those losers that robbed her and probably beat her to death. She is dead, do you want to look? So, all three went in the trailer and Worden carefully backtracked away. He went about a mile or so away that he could hold up for few days. He was familiar with the cave as he often stayed there when camping. It was secluded and almost impossible to recognize so it was what he needed now just to get lost. In the past he found some fruit crates and used them as shelves. He also has some provisions like pork and beans and some canned fruit. He would have plenty to eat. As it was when he got there everything was in order. He has the bread, and he opened a can of beans and dined like a king. To be earth shattering does not mean it has to take place hundreds of miles from its origin.

Lori stated before I get to my confession I am writing on a separate sheet of paper and thank you note to Mary Parks and Christie. We only met two or three times, but I was treated as a normal person not as a suspected murderer or worse. Before I begin, I would like to state my name is Lori Meeks and I am of sound mind and body. I am not being coerced by anyone to write of these events. We should have a beginning, so I think it probably started a few years back when Mrs. Meeks wrote to her sons to come to Germany and manage the boot and shoe manufacturing business. A short interval of time went by and she, Mrs. Meeks wrote and said that she was offered a fair share price for the business, so she decided to sell. Enclosed is a check to each son for fifty thousand dollars and she suggested the partner up and start a business. Food for thought so the three of us had a bone to chew on. We spoke with Mr. Jefferson and he proposed a cattle ranch in Mexico. He would loan us a substantial amount of money if the right land were found. So, the three of us went to Mexico we contacted land agent and we received quite a bit of response mostly not what we wanted. One property had all the necessary requirements we wanted to make an offer.

They had ten days to respond. It was fifty thousand acres with good soil, good water and close to a rail facility. We went back home, and I received a telephone call the offer was approved and whenever we got a chance to come to Mexico and do the paperwork. We were now or nearly so-called cattle ranchers. Then a bomb buster was dropped. Ralph said he wanted to kill and shoot Wordin. So, I said to him whoa! Think about what you just said. Ralph said that is all he was thinking about and he would do it tomorrow so I told Ralph to slow down, and we should think really clear about this. So, what prompted all of this? We were not having the usual affair. I never liked Ralph from a lover's standpoint. It was perplexing to say the least, but for no other reason than boredom I gave it some thought. So, I told Ralph very honestly that Worden and I were not madly in love, but I did not love you either meaning Ralph. Also, if you shoot him you would probably be suspect number one so what happens to little old Lori? If you are serious and work up a surefire scheme, then let us see if you have the guts to do it. So, I gave it some serious thought and came up with the conclusion that Worden and I were not going to make it and plus I figured a really good plan but having Ralph do this was a scary thought. He is not very strong, and he has all these allergies plus Worden is strong so there is only one chance to do this. So, I called Ralph and we would meet in the house where my father's sister lived. So, I told Ralph the plan and he said he liked it and he could do it. So, we both agreed okay let us do this. Here was the plan. Ralph was to go to Mexico legitimately pay his fee and not lose his receipt. She would pay Raul her father's helper five thousand dollars to get you out of Mexico and back in no legitimate route this time. If he were questioned it would show that he never left Mexico. They would wait for a rainy day and Ralph would slice Worden's head open. So, they waited, Lori paid the Mexican, Raul half of five thousand dollars and when he delivered Ralph back into Mexico, he would get the balance. That was a lot of money for Raul. The night they chose was raining but not badly it was mostly electric lightning and loud thundering noises. They left the stable door open so Wordin had no excuse to dismount but could drive right into his usual spot. The old horse was in his stall and he was in a frenzy fearing he would do so he kept banging against the makeshift door anxious to get out. Wordin's back was to Ralph but before he could execute him with the axe, the horse broke down the door. In its haste to get out of the barn he brushed up against Ralph who then lost control of his swing. As it went off, he hit Worden on the side of his head removing a big slice of head and cheek. Ralph tried for another blow but slipped in the water. Worden was dazed but not out, so he grabbed the axe handle and wrenched it out of Ralph hands and now he had the axe. Ralph started to run but was no match for Wordin who hit him in the ankle, so he fell. Then Worden turned the axe on Ralph and now Ralph was dead. Worden sat on a bale of straw. Lori came down from the loft and she was crying but not hysterically. Worden said, "So now I am a murderer, and you are an adulterous for life." "Go before I do something that I regret. "He put Ralph in the motorcycle, and he drove it outside this sprinkled corn all over and got the two pigs and let them eat the corn plus his sliced cheek and ear. He then would clean the axe and put it back in the barrel with the other tools. By morning there would be no evidence as the pigs were really gorging themselves and that was the last time, I would see Worden.

That was the end of Lori's confession. She carefully put it into an envelope and taped it shut. On the outside she wrote I give this to Mary Parks after she reads the content she can do as she wishes with it. Then she took another note pad and it said Mary there is an envelope for you on the coffee table. Goodbye and she placed this note near the door so Mary would see it. Then she called Mrs. Chum, Mr. Jefferson's housekeeper. She asked Mrs. Chum to wake Mary and come to her home and to bring Mr. Chum so he can be a witness.

Mary thanked Mrs. Chum and she and Mr. Chum went to Lori Meeks home. They found the note and retrieved the taped envelopes. Mary knocked on Lori's bedroom door but there was no answer, but the door was not locked. Mary entered and found Lori dead. Mary did not touch anything other than to take Lori's pulse. Mr. Chin would attest to that. Mary went back to Mr. Jefferson's house and gave Mr. Jefferson Lori's sealed envelopes. Worden has been holed up in the cave for some four days but instead of improving his medical problems are getting worse as he has no medicine to help him heal. Also, the pain is almost unbearable. When Worden left the cave, he had no real agenda. He is not out to kill so he is just at loose ends going because he knows he is going to die. The thought of being confined in a hospital is not the answer for him. It is still dark out and it is starting to rain again. So, he heads for the small strip mall that has a bakery and grocery and you might be able to find some day-old donuts or cakes or maybe some expired fruits. So, at the strip mall he bumps into a tall standalone scale for a moment he is startled that he grins and says his brother I have been looking for you? I want to ask you a question yes? If I kill someone in self-defense am I a murderer? Just then lights went on and Worden realize that he was talking to a scale. So, he went to the back of the store looks for some goodies. He found a bag and started loading it with bakery goods and the door to the bakery opened and someone said What are you doing? Get out of here or I will call the cops. Wordin answered okay okay I am leaving. So, he noticed a construction job that was shut down due to the bad weather. He found a pile of lumber covered by a black tarpaper and he crawled under in ate bakery goods and drank water. That was good he thought. He heard a motorcycle and thought he would try to find his friend, hop on, and maybe buy some transportation. His friend's shop was closed, but he would need to look close for it. It was still dark out, so he found is friend's shop and he would wait for him to open. His friend lived in a bedroom above the shop, and he would come down to make coffee. Good timing the light came on and he waited until he saw his friend, he could see him in the window and then rapped on the door. His friend motioned for him to come to the rear. The rear of the shop had an eight foot roll up garage door plus a conventional hinged door about three feet wide. So, Worden told him what he wanted, and he pulled out a wad of paper dollars. How much for this one? Sixteen hundred dollars. Sold said Worden and he gave money to the shopkeeper to count out. Worden did not think he could concentrate that long. So, the shopkeeper told Worden to take a spin on the bike as he had an important phone call to make. Worden threw five gallons can of gas in the sidecar and went to use the bath facilities walking by the door he heard his friend say yes, it is Worden. He was calling the police. Wordin took out his silence revolver and shot him in the head. He reacted despite area picked up the money from the desk and was gone. The place would be swarming with police in five minutes. Showing up there was at least five cars loaded with police. All they found was a dead shopkeeper. Worden by this time was miles away. So, the police set up roadblocks, but it was too late. Worden was long gone but he narrowed his chance of escaping by driving the sidecar motorcycle as there were that many on the road. Wordin was on his way to Mexico but a highway patrol car flashed red light. Worden ignored it in the cup put on his siren. Worden then made a quick U-turn before the cop figured it out Worden shot him dead. Christie was hidden in a grove of oleander bushes. Worden saw the side street and slowly went up that street to get off the freeway. Christie jumped out of the bushes and jumped on to Wharton's sidecar. Worden was trying to shake her off and pulled out his revolver to shoot her and as he did that, he lost control and raised his bike into a dozen trash cans where there was a construction site and he got out through a gate that was wide open, so Worden ran for it.

There was a large elevator that took material up and down the steel frame building. Wordin tried and he could not get it to move, so he finally figured the door had to be close and that was it. It started to head up. Meanwhile, Christie who was dazed saw the elevator going up and she ran and caught a steel beam and she maneuvered herself so that she would not fall. The elevator went up to about three or four floors when it stopped dead. Wordin opened the door and looked under and saw Christie. He blamed her for stalling the elevator so he managed to get a hold of a conduit in hand over hand he started to get Christie and knock her off the beam, but he figured he would shoot her, and he tried to get in a position to do so. It was difficult as he had to hang on to the conduit and try to shoot. He figured he was too far away, so he again started to advance hand over hand. He pulled out his revolver, but Christie pulled her gun out of her belly purse and took careful aim and shot the gun out of Worden's hand and she quickly put handcuffs on his wrist and shackled him to the conduit. She felt good now what do you say about that Mr. Worden as she laughed. She called Mary Parks and she told Mary to tell the captain to order the men not to shoot Worden as it would be murder. Christie told Mary that Worden was unconscious but not armed and he was handcuffed to a conduit. He needed immediate medical attention as his head was bleeding probably from the motorcycle crash. There was a loudspeaker proclaiming Lori Meeks dead, Lori Meeks confesses all over and over. Then two successive shots were heard, and Worden was dead shot in the heart while hanging by one arm. There was a heavy-duty crane with a large crow nest and the crowd asked was Sgt. Tim Forset a sharpshooter. He claimed his gun was never fired. He was waiting for orders to fire at will or witnesses said they saw three men leave the crow's nest and other witnesses said they saw two. One witness said she saw one. The sergeant said he was all alone. This story would go on forever. No one ever really knew who fired the fatal shot that killed Wordin. The loudspeaker kept blaring Lori Meeks dead Lori Meeks confesses all, Worden is shot by the sharpshooter and his dead.

Later Mary Parks and Christie said their goodbyes to Mr. Jefferson. Although Mary Parks and Christie solved most of the case. The district attorney said he was going to sue Mr. Jefferson for withholding information. Their claim is that Lori's confession is their property. Mr. Jefferson's attorney said it was Mr. Jefferson's property because he was given the confession that was taken by Mary Parks, a

Private Investigator who Mr. Jefferson had hired and paid personally.

The case went on as to who had the legal rights to the confession and the question as to who fatally shot and murdered Wordin. There were many unanswered questions, and the case is still a mystery and unsolved and we may never know the truth!

Is this the end for now?

Please watch for other Mary Parks,
private investigators books.